~ *Falling* ~

A novella by

Chris Bruce

For Amanda

'Our life passes in transformation.' (R. M. Rilke)

Contents

•

1.

A girl threw herself at my feet. Or rather, she tumbled to the ground where I stood, her nakedness evoking the original sinful fall. The event, like the passage of a comet, seemed to presage something.

She fell without warning from the all-too-collapsible chair, on which she had struggled (and failed) to remain immobile for fifty dawdling minutes. It was not the first time she had fallen asleep, to the annoyance of those in the group – the life class at the Academy of St Francis – whose procedure involved careful measurement. Her head would sag with slow reluctance towards her breastbone, only to spring back on first contact with the sternal hollow of her throat, the terminus of its slump where slumber threatened. A jolt then returned her to the original position, wearing an expression of unfeasible alertness: eyes wide open, interrogating the middle distance — and the clock located there. But this original set of the pose was if anything more disruptive to the measurers. It would be maintained only for a matter of seconds, before the eyes drooped and her head set out again on its path of decline, like a full moon that has overstayed the sunrise.

There was a lobby to fire Maria Pia from the life class. So far it had foundered on the inertia of the Head of the school. Umberto Pierangeli – Professor of Anatomical Drawing, to give him his title – was not one to shift, unless a deluge were lapping his feet, and then only with an elegant sidestep.

'But, boys and girls, she is so beautiful. For beauty we can forgive – a great deal, no?'

I was inclined to agree, but as a newcomer and extramural guest, my status in the class was probationary. I kept my own counsel.

The silence of the room – though not in truth silence, for there was the mechanical click accompanying each judder of the clock's second hand; there was the squeaky scratch of charcoal on paper; there was the vibration of a drawing board, as someone made urgent, wholesale erasures – this atmosphere of concentrated endeavour was ruptured (as I have described) at precisely seventeen minutes after midday.

The harsh scrape of chair legs and the sound of its collapsing weight, clattering the bare boards of the rostrum, caused me to look up: just in time to see Maria Pia still in mid-air, ungainly as a drunk, with an expression of bewilderment on her face. Her nudity was comical, undignified, like a soul judged and condemned for eternity to the circle of the absurd. And like those cascading deities that empty from baroque ceilings, she fell, coming to ground unstably and surely temporarily, on the very edge of the dais. I stepped forward, briefly fascinated by the compression of flesh on the angle of the podium. Her body, all akimbo, was offering to roll off its temporary ledge and fall the remaining distance to the floor. My intervention was untidy. I couldn't seize hold of her but I grasped the arm nearest to me, causing her to slew round and ground her feet, before the rest of her could follow. She regained some balance and dropped back, into a sitting position on the edge of the platform. I was still holding her arm, making sure she was steady. Her breast jammed against my hand, its touch warm and without resistance. Self-consciously, I let go.

Now there was a crowd around her – the whole room had been sucked to where she sat. Maria Pia looked dazed. She was trying to speak. Her utterances were fragmentary

'Such a stupid cow... I don't know what...did I faint?...'

Someone had a hand on her brow, feeling her temperature. Her nakedness now seemed improper and pleaded to be covered. Her wrap materialised and was draped around her shoulders.

Time was called on the class, with ten minutes left to go. There was still a melee in attendance. I picked up my belongings, and went out into the sun.

After the enclosed atmosphere, the sensation of heat and the strong, sharp light were welcome, even delicious. I noticed my hand was shaking a little. It was still early. I decided to hang around and set myself down on the kerb.

The street was narrow, populated, at pavement level, by artisans' workshops and small shops. Opposite me, where I sat, was some kind of metal worker's. The interior, to my view, appeared almost pitch black; there was probably someone inside that I couldn't see, labouring at a bench.

'I have to thank you. I don't know your name.' The voice came from behind me. I turned to respond.

'Adam,' I said.

'Adam. That's significant, don't you think?'

'My mother thought so…'

'Yes, but that's not what I meant…' Maria Pia still looked pale. Her face was an oval, like a Modigliani woman. Her hair, between blond and brown in colour, was down now, as she normally wore it when not modelling. She parted it down the middle of her head; it was long, hanging in ringlets, well below her shoulders. She sat down next to me and, in an automatic sort of way, extracted the elements to roll a cigarette from the blanket bag slung across her shoulder.

'What I mean is…well a fall…it's something particular. Out of the ordinary. I looked for it on my life line.' She held up her palm so I could see it. 'See, there's a little line that crosses it. There!' She pointed with her other hand. 'Can you see? It means something…' She shrugged in a way that implied an infinity of interpretations.

I looked, but I could not see. I am an unrewarding subject in matters spiritual and I was probably looking at the wrong line. Her hands had a delicacy that I had always enjoyed when I was drawing her. Her fingers were fine, a quality accentuated by her nails; these she maintained long, painting them turquoise.

'What does it mean?' I asked, not sure whether she was serious or making some sort of roundabout joke.

'It means a change. And you are called Adam. That is important on a symbolical level…or is it symbolic, I don't know…'

'Symbolic, I think. You mean 'the fall of man' and all that…' This wasn't the first time in my life that my name had provided material for double entendres. I was resigned to it.

'Yes. You see! You do see…' Her tone was more animated now that she felt I was getting on her wavelength. 'But…' She paused and looked directly at me. 'But you were the one who prevented the fall, not like in the Bible when…you know. It's all upside-down from the way it's supposed to be. You get that, don't you?'

'You were the one upside-down.'

She flushed slightly, perhaps considering her inversion. 'Yes, I was the one upside-down. And it was fallen Adam that caught me and turned me the right way. It's the opposite to the way you'd think...' She detected that my willingness to comprehend was faltering. 'It means something important, anyway. It means a change,' she said, finishing on a categoric note.

Maria Pia had rolled her cigarette by now and lit it with her Zippo. We sat on the kerb, absorbing the sunlight, squinting into the dazzle of the sky. She took deep drags on the cigarette. Its smoke drifted tantalisingly my way. I had recently quit, part of my reappraisal of myself since I had begun a new job. A man in a buff storeman's coat emerged from the black void opposite, the place that made metal fixings: Vulcan summoned by Apollo. Lunchtime was approaching.

'I want you to help me with one of my tableaux. I want to do "The Fall". It would need you. You would have to be in it...'

She went on to explain that she liked to take photographs of groups of friends and members of her family, in staged compositions. She had a Rolleiflex and lighting equipment. It was evidently quite professional – not the casual snapshot photography I was versed in. There was something about Maria Pia that was hard to turn down. Her way of asking made you feel as though you had been entrusted with her entire happiness. I said I would like to see some of her pictures.

'I'll bring some next class. I'm modelling again then. But you *will* help me, won't you? It's necessary, for you too, I think...' She gave a smile that was winning and, at the same time, had a hint of fairground guile to it. 'My photographs are like journeys, to find things out...truths that we keep hidden...' She smiled again, a smile that seemed certain of itself. I hadn't a clue what she meant, but I was getting used to the idea that much of what she said was off my frequency. I was remembering the touch of her breast. We stood up, exchanged friendship kisses, and went our separate ways.

2.

By the time I caught up with Maria Pia again, I had forgotten about her project but the subject came up nonetheless. She seemed anxious to resurrect the idea.

We met in the street. She was with a young man in his twenties, a little older than her. There was a family resemblance: the same almond-shaped face, the same grave eyes. He was her brother, Matteo. As we walked, Maria Pia dived into a shop leaving the pair of us outside and feeling awkward.

It appeared she had told the story of the fall incident back at home.

'It was lucky you were on hand. She could have been hurt,' he said, to break the ice. We shuffled our feet as we awaited her return.

'Maria Pia doesn't believe in luck.'

'No, no, we mustn't say that!' Matteo laughed. He was more of an empiricist than his sister. He told me he was in his final year at the medicine faculty. 'Of course, let's say it was providential. Who knows, maybe it is "all in the stars". The deeper truth of things is buried below the surface – I think we can all agree on that, at least.' His own field of interest was Psychiatry, in which he planned to specialise.

~ o ~

The next occasion I saw Maria Pia was at class. She came over to me as I was setting up.

'I've got some of my photographs to show you. I hope you have time afterwards.'

I wanted to explain that I'd made arrangements, I had to be away promptly from the session, but her look implied that if I said 'no', the disappointment would be irremediable.

I said, 'I've got to meet some friends. We're going to get lunch at Rocco's Counter, and eat in the square. You'd be welcome. They'd like to see your photographs. I've told them about your work.' This was a lie. I would have to manage it when we all got together. She hesitated.

'I don't show my photographs, except to people who know me. They are personal – it's difficult to explain. But OK – it's your friends.'

As she turned away, she darted me a bruised look, as if I'd betrayed a trust. It was time to begin the session. She shrugged the robe off and mounted the podium. The pose she adopted gave me a back view of her, partly obscured by the chair. It was a dull angle to draw.

~ o ~

We were late meeting Laura and Danny. They had already bought their food and were sitting under a plane tree facing the fountain, a hexagonal basin into which a writhing knot of mythical fish spurted water. The midday *pausa* was falling like a curfew. A couple of restaurants, at the entrance to the square, were in full swing. Residents of the surrounding buildings were drifting back for lunch indoors. One or two groups of men lingered by the herd of parked-up scooters, to argue the toss or maybe haggle over a deal. Danny and Laura had begun to eat. Pigeons were showing interest, trying to calibrate the safe distance at which to prospect for crumbs.

I introduced Maria Pia; I had previously recounted the fall, the accident averted. Laura asked, out of politeness, if that morning had been mishap-free. Danny was tongue-tied in the presence of a girl he didn't know. He was working late shifts in a restaurant, washing up. It was drudgery but he took it in his stride. The only complaint I'd heard him voice was that he missed going to see the Arsenal, now that the season was underway.

I could see that Danny was fascinated by Maria Pia, even though he remained largely silent and left the conversation to the three of us. She herself was shy, taking stock of the company, but her shyness had a winsome quality to it. Her remarks laid trails of incomplete information; floated quirky opinions that depended on no reasoning for their existence. She invited interrogation, yet met the simplest enquiries with a coyness that suggested she were on the verge of divulging secrets.

After we had eaten I mentioned the photographs that she had brought. She displayed a reluctance, wholly feigned I felt sure.

'I don't know (she pronounced the "k") whether I should let you see, whether you would like them…'

'Well, the only way to tell – is to show them,' I said, determined to jolly things along.

'Yes, I k-know.' She hid her face in her hands like a child playing hide and seek, counting the allotted time, before calling 'coming, ready or not' and going directly to the usual hide-outs, the ones used on many previous occasions. 'All the same, they are quite…strange…'

'Well, if you don't want to show them…but I thought the idea was to do your project, "The Fall"?'

'Yes…but now I don't k-know…'

'But now you've said they are strange, we are curious…but perhaps you think we couldn't handle the strangeness – oh, I get it – you think we are too square!' I found myself playing her game, even though now I didn't really care whether she showed the pictures.

'No, no, you are not square…but these photographs are like part of me… I don't want you to not like me, that's all.'

She had taken the photographs out of her bag before she had finished saying this. They were in a small portfolio tied with a leather thong. It would have been easy, after the preamble, to show just me: after all, that had been the deal originally. Laura and Danny had taken Maria Pia at her word and struck up their own conversation. However, she repositioned herself in the middle of the three of us, and opened the folder. After the show of reticence, all constraints now were gone, it seemed. She systematically laid the pictures in a group on the ground. There were ten, each mounted in a black card frame.

Despite her tiresome shilly-shallying, as soon as we saw them, we were enchanted. The compositions were, in a sense, what I had been led to believe: Maria Pia and an ensemble of young people, posing. Yet, her tableaux, whilst enacting classical or baroque subjects, had the air of being clipped from reality. The moments could have equally been the aftermath of a party: young bodies languid from recent waking; blank expressions guarding private thoughts, whilst holding station in attitudes that Maria Pia had devised. In a way, maybe, the compositions were a window on the reality of the life model: the human prop, mind otherwise engaged. Among the

12

players, I recognised Matteo.

For all their protagonists' dead-panning, or because of it perhaps, the pictures were ravishing. The lighting was expert, lingering over the texture of skin, describing features, defining physiques; and the colour was rich, like nothing that ever came back from Boots. The company was attired in a motley of fancy dress, evening gowns, old corduroy pants, velvet bits and pieces, chosen it appeared for the sumptuousness of their colours and surfaces. Often the actors wore drapery like classical deities, whimsically combined with burlesque undergarments. Maria Pia most frequently appeared like this, except in one or two compositions where she was naked.

One tableau presented a reworking of *Susanna and the Elders*: Maria Pia plays Susanna; she stands passively, clothes discarded, at the mercy of four men, young men in this case, who form a semi-circle around her. They appear to be engaged in a ritual dance; their forms blurred and they are making lewd, hostile-seeming gestures. Their concealment, traditional in the treatment of the subject, comes in the form of caricature masks: a Devil, a Frankenstein, a werewolf and a Richard Nixon.

Not all the scenes were as frankly menacing as this one. One was a *Pietà*. Maria Pia lies horizontally, her head angling downwards, across the lap of Matteo. He looks the man of science: he is wearing horn-rimmed glasses, and a dark suit. Maria Pia is naked in this tableau too; the lighting has contrived to illuminate her torso and leave her features in shadow.

Laura was looking intently at the photographs. 'These are wonderful,' she said. It was clear from her voice that she meant what she said. 'Is that Diana and Actaeon?' It was a set-up in a grandly dishevelled bathroom. A group of girls are ministering to Maria Pia, towelling her hair, painting her nails. They look quizzically at a boy who has entered, carrying a comically small bow and arrow tipped with a rubber sucker.

Maria Pia seemed glad of the good notices, though I guessed this was not the first time her work had garnered plaudits; her photographs were impressive beyond any dispute. Laura began picking out details and asking how she had realised them. Maria Pia told us that she had the run of an old house that belonged to her grandparents. In the past it had stood in countryside, but the peripheries of the city had expanded and enveloped it.

Later, even these newcomers had given way to the modern apartment buildings that now surrounded the place. The grandparents had raised their family in it and, later, Maria Pia and her siblings. Now, they had moved out and gone to live in an apartment. Maria Pia used the place as her *Petit Trianon*. It was the location for her pieces; lights and camera were always set up.

As we continued to look at the photographs, I noticed Danny. Maria Pia's photo-compositions appeared to be an epiphany for him: they held his interest as no art in this city of art treasures had managed to do. Part of his fascination was undoubtedly Maria Pia's nudity. When we had roomed together, I'd discovered him to be quite puritanical. I had never asked him directly, but I surmised he was a virgin. He didn't have a stash of *Mayfair* and *Penthouse* in his bedside drawer, still less the Danish material that Luca passed around. I guessed he found her nakedness in the photographs perturbing. All the same, I think what mesmerised him most of all was the assurance of Maria Pia, unabashed at allowing us sight of her alter self.

After a time we broke up. I had a lesson to teach. Laura and Maria Pia, I noticed, went off together, still deep in conversation. I realised that Maria Pia was now part of our life here.

3.

I didn't see Danny again until later that evening. My life was growing complicated at this time; a far cry from earlier days in the city when, as summer students, he and I had shared a room. I lived now with my girlfriend, Daisy. We had a flat. It was meant to be wonderful but things were not going well between us. Daisy was nocturnal: she had a job in a club, where she worked until the early hours. In the meantime, I was teaching English, working regular hours. The result was that our encounters were becoming more and more infrequent.

My habit was to seek out Danny for company; we would stay up and talk when he came back after his shift. Usually he had stories from work: the fellow *plongeur* who had tamed a rat; the romance between Annalisa, the waitress, and one of the regular customers. That night, we began in that vein and then, suddenly, he said, 'Y'know Maria Pia – d'you think I've got a chance?'

'What sort of chance? Romantically, you mean?' It was a dumb rejoinder, because that was obviously what he meant, but I was trying hard to think of an answer that would not be an absolute crusher. He had no hope at all, as far as I could see.

'Yeah. It's daft, isn't it? I mean, what would I do? Ask her to the flicks? See if she wants to check out my record collection, well, Robin's collection, that is…'

'Maybe she'd like to hear you play the guitar? You're getting good now…'

'That's a good point! I could tidy up some of my pieces.' He brightened at this idea. After a moment's reflection he resumed, 'The thing is, I'm no good with girls – just too bumbling around them. But, y'know, I get where she's at, with her photos I mean. It's what we're like when the lid comes off – what we're all like, that is. I feel I could talk to her…' He fell silent again. I felt awkward. What he was saying seemed implausible, and yet I could see Maria Pia lapping up the mooning devotion of which I guessed him capable.

He began again. 'Sometimes unlikely blokes pull great women, don't they? Like, if it's really important, if they're determined, if they can show them it's important, the women I mean...'

I didn't respond. I was of the belief that his scenario only came true if the unlikely bloke in question was rich.

He went on. '...the thing is, I think this is important. I've got this feeling, this kind of certainty. It's ridiculous just talking like this...it's just that I think – I mean, I know – something is going to *happen* with this girl...'

Some people describe love at first sight like this. They say, 'I knew straight away this was the woman I would marry'. Usually, it seemed to me, these annunciations of the unconscious arrive after many other, more typical encounters with women; edited from such stories are the part where the woman in question says 'drop dead'.

We decided to call it a night. When I got back home, I lay in bed finding sleep elusive. Danny's confession had left me unsettled. Since the incident of the fall, I had been at pains not to confront a new feeling I had; the notion that in time something would develop with Maria Pia — and me. It had taken up residence as a piece of secret knowledge, subterranean and separate from my daily existence. I preferred to avoid a bald acknowledgement of it; it meant I was 'looking around'.

As I lay there, I began to replay recent conversations with Daisy, or rather the continuous, rolling conversation that now seemed to surface, whenever we went to the palace gardens opposite our flat, to idle on a shaded bench, as tourists laboured up to the panoramic terrace; or to the nondescript church that housed a fresco sequence I never tired of (it was more my thing than Daisy's); or to the Lido where we spent our Sunday afternoons, sunbathing on the grass, Daisy in a white bikini like Ursula Andress (the Lido was definitely her element). This conversation picked up at times and in places where we'd once been happy to simply abide. It seemed to me that we were prospecting for a way to end things. For example, we had aired, in very hypothetical terms, the idea of an open relationship. Once launched, the topic leads quickly and inevitably to other questions, too promptly denied – 'So, is there anyone…you know…anyone you could be attracted to?' It felt as though, having set up home in our flat, we were chafing against the fixity proposed by our situation.

The year was 1969, the year of Woodstock; the year after the Sorbonne students took over Paris; eighteen months after the Prague Spring. In principle, both of us thought exclusivity a stifling bourgeois construct (albeit our love had been a conventional boy-meets-girl romance). We venerated openness, spontaneity and self-expression; these were the dues you paid when you swam in the stream of radicalism. As Daisy said, 'Just because you're with someone doesn't mean you can't make connections…basically fancy other…women in your case. I understand that.'

I understood that she was referring to herself; she received a lot of attention from men at the club. It was her job to encourage free spending with calculated flirtation. Although she referred to the guys as "creeps", I knew she enjoyed the work; not all of the guys were creeps.

Unlike Danny, I wasn't smitten by Maria Pia, except in that literal fashion, when she tumbled and we had collided. I had nevertheless grown used to the expectation that we would have further tumbles, further explorations of the horizontal. But now that Danny had made his declaration, such a view of the future needed an overhaul. The idea of vying for Maria Pia's affections was grotesque. Danny was a novice as far as women were concerned. Also there was the matter of his being my mate – I wasn't going to queer his pitch, was I? I would stand back, let him make his play, whatever it might be. But his gauche calf love irritated; it niggled that Danny hadn't stopped to consider whether I might have designs – prior designs, since I had known Maria Pia for some weeks…and he had just met her…thanks to my introducing him… OK – as far as he knew, Daisy and I were set…but he could have asked…

Inner voices chattered on in this vein for a while. Something else then struck me a hammer blow: when, I wondered, had I become someone who sets out to sleep with women who hardly interest them?

~ o ~

I dozed, only to be awoken by Daisy's presence. It must have been 5 o'clock: daylight was seeping through the shutters of our room. She was moving with extreme care in order not to wake me. Perhaps she was desperate to get some shut-eye, or – I lay wondering – was her stealth in order to avoid questions? She was late home.

I maintained the pretence of sleep and watched as she removed her clothes, laying them to rest over a wooden chair. Last of all, she looped her knickers lopsidedly over the chair back, where they hung like a wilted leaf. In the dull, pewter light she looked sleek, as if having emerged from water. I noted, almost in surprise, her womanliness: the vigour in her hips, normally hidden by loose clothing or rendered banal by the cocktail dress she wore to work. She stretched, both arms reaching upwards, her back arched, until, abruptly, she let go of the tension and her whole being slackened; she rounded herself and scurried under the bedsheet.

I moved to give her room, making clear I was now awake. Daisy's back was towards me. I touched her shoulder, wondering whether I should let her feel my erection. Proposing love-making, when she came back from work, had a chequered history; fine in the early days but unwelcome more recently. I brushed against her rear. She tensed for a moment before relaxing and half turning her head. We kissed. Perhaps, like me, she'd calculated the time since we'd last had sex. She rolled back on her stomach, knowing I liked to take her from behind. Perhaps she'd reflected that repairs were in order; she also knew that we'd be quick that way.

4.

Subsequent events gathered a momentum that was out of my control. Laura had befriended Maria Pia. She was full of enthusiasm for her work, and wanted to take part in the making. They discussed ideas. Danny too contrived to join them as they made those plans. Maria Pia seemed to find him amusing. She had evolved the mannerism of ruffling his mop of spaniel curls at periodic intervals, something he enjoyed and seemed to invite, holding his head at a distance and height that made it easy for her.

One evening, I was with Laura in a bar. We were watching the throng outside on the pavement. It was a Friday, still early, and people were strolling with an air of contentment, excitement in some cases. The weekend was here and a night out was getting ready to begin. Laura and I had not long been in jobs. This rhythm was new to us. It felt good. The prospect of the break from work unfurled before us like fresh white sheets, a luxurious emptiness. As we talked, however, I got the sense that Laura already had plans. When I probed, she told me that Maria Pia was organising a séance.

'What do you mean? A séance to contact the dead…?'

'No no, not quite like that. It's really just her word for a sort of happening…'

'Happening?' It sounded like more of Maria Pia's kooky mysticism. I wanted to be scornful.

'Well, it's how she gets to take her photographs,' Laura explained. 'She's not like a film director, just bossing everyone around, like the big brain with the big idea – a puppeteer manipulating the actors, you know, that sort of thing.'

'I didn't really imagine that…' I said, wondering all the same how it had come about that Laura was now party to Maria Pia's inner secrets. I was completely out of touch by the sound of it.

'It's more spontaneous, more exciting. She has her idea, but then she needs to find it again, in whatever happens,' Laura explained, sounding assured and versed in what she was describing. 'She gets a kind of party together, and everyone sort of…hangs out…has fun…talks about stuff.' She gestured in the air with her lighted cigarette. 'Serious kinds of stuff – it's going to be all weekend. You're coming along, aren't you? I was asked to tell you.'

'Sure,' I said, wondering why Maria Pia hadn't told me herself. She and I had sat chatting together in the street, a couple of days previously. The whole idea must have been very spontaneous indeed; she'd made no mention of it.

I agreed to go, from pique at being left out rather than real interest in the séance. If I was truthful, I was beginning to find Maria Pia quite irritating, with her constant ploys to snare your curiosity. All the same, when you boiled it down, this was a party and despite myself, I was – yes – curious. The topic dropped. Laura and I decided to spend some of our wages on a sit-down meal, to enjoy the novelty of solvency to the full.

5.

We were due at Maria Pia's the following afternoon. Danny told me he was nervous with anticipation, so much so he'd almost been sick. Maria Pia had made a point of saying that she needed him to be there; I guessed she'd rewarded him with several touslings when he agreed to juggle his shifts to make it. We'd brought some food and wine at our hostess's behest. Sitting on the bus, our carriers jiggled on the floorboards. We could almost have passed for a family on a picnic excursion: watching the unfamiliar surroundings spool by, slightly anxious should we miss our stop.

The house, sole survivor of what had once been an elegant neighbourhood, was a stucco building rising four stories to a shallow-pitched terracotta roof of the kind characteristic in older parts of the city. To either side was open ground, disused since the post-war clearance. The doorway was a coaching entrance. Above the usual signs – *Polite Notice, No Parking* and *Cave Canem* – someone had graffitied, *A bas le travail* and *Tune in*; perching on top of the 'T' they had painted a red cockerel. One of the pair of coach-house doors was slightly ajar.

I had gone with Daisy. The séance would be a welcome distraction for both of us. We walked in silence through the gate, following Laura and Danny into a courtyard behind the house. This weekend was Danny's chance to press his suit: 'get the ball in the net', as he put it. Daisy and I were here to give support – and to see if this love story would turn out better than our own.

I recognised a number of our fellow guests from Maria Pia's photographs: there was 'Actaeon' of the toy bow and arrow, and the chorus of 'Nereids', like perennial bridesmaids, and one or two faces from the drawing class. I noticed her brother Matteo, and a slim, diffident girl, whom I later discovered to be Maria Pia's sister, Agata. There were a number of others I'd never seen, including a short man with an oversized head and a mane of blond-streaked hair; he was tendering a tray of drinks. Perhaps in keeping with his butling duties, he was wearing knee breeches but, in acknowledgment of the warm afternoon sun, he was shirtless and wore flip-flops on his feet. Seeing us he came over with the tray.

'Hello, I'm Casanova,' he announced, rolling his eyes like a ham actor.

'I'm Adam,' I said. The others were still trying to decide what to make of him, so I introduced them. 'This is Laura, and Danny.'

'The Original Sinner, and...the Muse, most welcome...and,' he looked at Danny, '...the Troubadour.' Apparently we could not just be ourselves.

'...and this is Daisy.'

For Daisy, he effused an 'enchant-ay' and attempted a kiss of the hand, which she turned back into a handshake. Daisy was not fond of 'smarm'.

Undeterred, Casanova made a courtly gesture indicating the goings-on behind him. 'We are preparing a *mise en scène*. Come and see.'

Across the yard, I noticed Maria Pia for the first time. She was moving lights around, powerful ones on stands, the kind you might expect in a TV studio. Meanwhile a construction was taking shape under the biggest tree in the courtyard, a Mediterranean pine with distinguished trunk and undulating boughs. A long table had been placed there, with an assortment of seating: formal dining chairs, camp-stools, plastic chairs and a unicycle, propped at a chaotic angle like a wasted drunk. There was a lot of drapery around, some suspended from the branches to form a canopy, some shrouding an arrangement of crates behind the table, crudely representing the geometric topography of Renaissance paintings.

'The project is to make the "Five Senses". It's a traditional subject; there's a Rubens series, for example.' Laura, evidently *au courant*, offered this information. The 'Fall' idea of early days seemed to have been discarded.

The tableau in construction was obviously going to be 'Taste'. The table was covered with a cloth, a fine piece of lace-bordered linen; it properly belonged in a chest of best things, reserved for the festivities – unions, christenings, homecomings – that marked the progress of solidly rooted lives, as well, of course, as their final passing.

Food was starting to be laid out. In fact someone had gone to a lot of trouble: plates of pastries, cuts of meat, quiches, tarts, crostini, frittatas, sauces, earthy stews, vibrant salads, all issued from the interior of the house. We pitched into the work of transporting the feast from the kitchen, where it was mustered in readiness, joining in with the gang of volunteers who formed an improvised but efficient human conveyor into the courtyard. Our own offering – a couple of baguettes and some cream cheese – seemed footling beside the rich board being assembled. We contrived to leave it indoors, apologetic and half hidden behind a cluster of wine bottles.

6.

Maria Pia was fussing, composing the table like a still life, pausing every so often to take a picture with a Polaroid, slung correspondent-style around her neck. She took her time. I wished she would hurry: the sight of the food and the handling of it had left me ravenous; I guessed the same was true of the others too.

'What can we really know? Do we know anything at all? For sure?' It was Matteo, proceeding like an evangelist through the troop of us standing ready to descend on the feast. 'Everything we know or believe comes from our senses – but our senses, do they really tell us the truth? Can we trust them?' Following in his wake like an altar boy was Casanova, still bearing a tray of drinks that he dispensed as they wended through the group. There was the air of zealots about both of them. The drinks were small shots of brightly coloured syrups (it seemed like); some were vivid red like Campari, some green like mint syrup or blue like sapphire. I guessed this was an idea they had come up with for Maria Pia's photography. The drinks had been poured into a variety of second-hand glasses, none alike. In the sun the tray sparkled like a hoard of jewels. People were downing their shots; something about the drinks made them smile.

Matteo had reached us. He handed across a couple of glasses. 'Try my prescription – I am *nearly* a doctor, after all! Give yourself to the unexpected. Experience is stranger than you imagine. Not-knowing is real; not-knowing is the only truth. Open your mind, embrace uncertainty, expand…' He was almost intoning. Were it not for an ironical smile as he spoke, the whole performance would have seemed ridiculous. Casanova gave his trademark gurn. He *was* ridiculous: a calculated buffoon in his knee breeches, now complemented by a top hat, a bit like the Mad Hatter. He handed Danny a glass, this one with a chartreuse-coloured liquid.

We hesitated a moment, bilious-looking drinks in hand, then Danny muttered, 'Oh well…' and with a toasting gesture drank his in one go. He stood blinking for a moment, then he too began to laugh.

'Oh, that's so weird. That's really weird. You've got to try that!'

We were curious now, and took the plunge with our drinks, unsure what to expect. Mine was one of the blue ones. It looked as if it would taste like toothpaste.

The drink was not in the least syrupy, but light like champagne and, once swallowed, the taste lingered on your tongue. And the taste – at first you couldn't tell what it was, except there was none of the expected minty bite. Then, gradually, a flavour formed. It configured like a shape emerging from mist – into prawns? – no, it was still developing, growing in presence as if it were gas filling a space – chicken? – no – suckling pig? – no – but there was an odour of chargrill, almost – and wild sage – and then it was gone, just the merest brothy scent – the proximity of a girl on a hot afternoon – then, nothing.

'That's brilliant,' said Laura, the delight of a child at Christmas on her face. 'So many flavours and fragrances, like a pharmacy – aniseed, camphor, pear drops...' Her drink had been blue like mine, yet it had clearly been different. Unlike the others, I had not drunk mine in one go. I was about to finish it but, when I looked down, I saw a fly had landed on the surface; a large unsavoury fly, recently flown in from Turdville and now fancying to rinse down its last ripe ingestions with a drop of the blue. I wondered what it would make of Matteo's remedy for uptight normalcy. I put the glass down and left Mr Fly to drink its fill.

There was an atmosphere of festivity as we pressed forward to the table in a good-natured stampede. There were plates, but nothing in the way of eating implements. Much of the food was designed for a buffet, so most simply loaded their plates and either stood around, as at a cocktail party, or found a place to sit. It was the height of the afternoon. The yard was sheltered. The bright chill of the morning had given way to fulsome, gilded warmth, in which we bathed and lolled. Time drifted deliciously.

I found myself sitting next to the quiet-looking girl I'd noticed when we first arrived. I introduced myself.

'I met Maria Pia at drawing class. I'm Adam. It was me who caught her when she had her fall...'

'Yes, I know who you are. Maria Pia told me about you. I'm Agata. I'm Maria's sister.'

'She did?' I guessed Maria Pia must have regaled her whole family with the incident: Matteo had known all about it when I met him.

'Yes, but not just that – other things too.' I wondered what the other things could amount to but, at that moment, our attention was taken by a confusion of voices, growing more excitable.

There was an argument about what to do and how to do it. Around the table, Maria Pia had arranged a group of eight or ten banqueters. They were her regular players whom, in most cases, I recognised from her photographs. Several wore items of costume – uniform hats, capes, shifts – but since others were wearing kaftans, or patchwork jackets, and a lot of beads, distinctions between fancy dress and regular attire were impossible to draw. Casanova was among the group. I noticed Daisy had joined them.

A girl was climbing onto the table, encouraged by urgings – 'Go on, get up, *forza*, hup…' Helping hands steadied her on the flimsy rush chair she was using to ascend. A practically minded guy was trying to fix a wobbly table leg. He was wearing a brass helmet that slipped every time he looked down, impeding his work. This struck me as extremely funny indeed.

'That's Mariuccia,' I heard Agata saying, an edge of disapproval in her voice. ' You could bet she'd be the one getting up there – she's an exhibitionist.' Her assessment seemed accurate. Mariuccia was taking clothes off, though not like a striptease but more in the way of an athlete shedding track-suiting. I turned back to look at Agata. Her quiet demeanour was deceptive. She seemed to have a toughness to her and a practicality. I wondered what she was thinking about the happening getting underway around us.

Someone struck up a guitar. I recognised the guy. He was a regular busker around the city; he did a passable James Taylor. Mariuccia was in her knickers, moving loosely to the music, arms swaying above her head. The other players were configured around her in a Last Supper kind of formation, although Actaeon had now joined her on the table. I found myself observing Matteo who was patrolling the perimeter of the table group, taking no part but absorbed in the action, like a football coach on the touchline.

As I watched, Daisy climbed onto the table with the others. Her face was flushed.

'Those drinks were crazy. Who came up with them?' I felt curious to get to the bottom of something; there were things I was missing. Agata was a straight talker. Perhaps she could help me figure out the thing, whatever it was, that was passing me by.

'The drinks? That was Matteo. He likes to mystify. When we were smaller, he used to entertain us with magic tricks. He was really good at them. Maria Pia used to like to dress up, to make theatre, you know – and Matteo was the conjurer, the illusionist. They were always putting on little shows, like now – this is their show, we are all part of it – but...' she gestured to the table crowd, 'they don't all realise.' Some of them were eating from the dishes that were set out, wolfing the food like starving pets. Maria Pia was beginning to take pictures, standing behind the Roleiflex on its tripod.

'So the drinks were one of his tricks?' I was watching Daisy dancing. The (now) three women on the table were making moves as if they were performing in *Hair*. Just like Mariuccia, Daisy had stripped down to her briefs and was laughing. I wanted to get her to come down, but I had never seen her happier.

'Yes, they are his party piece, you could say.' Agatha was answering me. She gave a hard little laugh, then continued more matter-of-factly. 'He is a chemist. Before he transferred to the medicine faculty, he studied Chemistry. He likes to play around. He can get flavourings and colours – you know – always to mystify, to mystify...'

The busker guy was bashing out a driving rhythm on the guitar. A girl with maracas had joined in. The sounds seemed to hang in the air. It was only a battered acoustic guitar but the music echoed and accumulated, layer upon layer until it was overwhelming like an avalanche. I wondered how he did it.

Some time passed.

The antics of the crowd around the table grew wilder. Casanova had smeared himself with tomato sauce and face-painted some of the others. Daisy was in there, somewhere. They were now licking each other down and food was being thrown. One of the girls had custard-pied herself with a flan. Mariuccia lay on the table like the centrepiece of the banquet.

Danny having cast himself as first grip, was busy helping Maria Pia loading and moving the camera. Between shots they stood face to face in an embrace, foreheads touching. He had obviously made his move. It was Maria Pia who terminated these interludes. I guessed she wanted to get back to the camera. The players of the tableau were getting progressively more carnal in their theatrics. Casanova was mugging for the camera, slobbering food from Mariuccia's surfaces like a cannibal. She had turned into an over-excited child, laughing and squealing uncontrollably. Her breasts – or they could've been Daisy's breasts – jiggled. The rolling, shifting mass of bodies filled the entire frame of my vision; their movements slowed and, as I watched, appeared to synchronise with the dirging note of the guitar, which strangely was playing just one chord: strum stram, strum stram, wham bam, wham bam, whip whup, hup, hup, hup…

7.

'We don't have to stay out here. You can see the way it's going to go. Maria Pia is getting what she wanted...' Agata's words seemed to come from a distance, even though she was speaking into my ear.

'We don't *have* to stay...' I echoed, wondering why dumbly repeating her words seemed to bring new significance to them.

'Come, I'll show you around the house...' said Agata, standing up and reaching for my hand as if she were suddenly my older sister. We walked inside, or rather 'inside' peeled back, then wrapped itself around us. She took me through rooms that were mostly empty, or had one or two bits of bric-a-brac in them. Their vacancy preserved and amplified our footsteps. We played hide and seek, then we were kissing.

We went to her room. It was at the top of the house. I stumbled on the stairs several times, causing Agata to stop and help me to my feet, because having fallen, I was inclined to stay where I was. Her room was small, a Romany's caravan, the walls lined with hangings. The sound of the others fell away as the door closed. Our breathing, its rising cadence, filled the space and contained us like swaddling. She straddled me and we fucked. What we did was slow, very slow; the merging of us seemed to be a place we had come to dwell.

When I awoke the room seemed bigger than I remembered it. Agata was awake. In fact I had kept her awake, calling out in my sleep and thrashing around in the narrow bed. I could remember dreams that were intensely coloured but I couldn't begin to recount any of them. I said I was feeling thirsty.

'That's probably the LSD,' said Agata. I must have looked nonplussed. 'You didn't realise?'

No, I had not. Something in my brain got stuck on pounds, shillings and pence; there'd been a robbery? Surely that was what she meant? My experience of drugs went as far as sharing a joint at a party. LSD was quite a new thing. I knew it was serious: it meant dicing with your mind, stepping into the unknown, a decision not taken lightly. I began to feel panicked at the idea I'd been mickeyed.

'It's OK,' she said. 'You'll come down. It's OK. It's beautiful when you feel good with someone. I'll look out for you.' I detected again the steady practicality in her voice. I gave in to it; she was in control. There was nothing really to get scared about. We drew ourselves into an embrace; Agata's face became a massive cinematic close-up.

A while later, I asked, 'LSD? What's the deal? I didn't know.' I hoped my voice was steady. The words came from outside somewhere. They had a smell, earthy, or was that us, our sweat? I wondered when the strangeness of everything would end. I was bored with it – and stuck in it.

'Matteo's drinks…? I told you he was a chemist. He knows how to make it. Maria Pia's séances are like an experiment for him. He even makes notes about them…'

'Did you take some?'

'No, I don't take it any more.' Her face clouded as she said this. She literally became tight-lipped. I inferred that it was not always 'OK'. I felt a warm flush of gratitude, of peace. She had looked out for me, as she had said. The feeling grew into something strong, like singing, high and pure in the distance. I felt like walking around, and still that thirst, an insistent presence.

'I'm going to get some water.' Agata looked at me, I think trying to read whether I was capable. 'It's fine. I'll be back in a minute.' I got dressed and went out.

8.

I could still hear the singing. It was strangely pitched, between melody and chant. I realised it was coming from the floor below. I went downstairs, following the sound. There was a corridor off the landing. I stumbled to the end of it and opened a door. The sight that confronted me was of Maria Pia almost completely covered in spatters of paint, without which she would have been naked. She was oblivious of my entry, but remained intent on her purpose – which was daubing a vast sheet – a canvas – spread out on the floor. She was walking its perimeter in a sort of stalking motion, as if sneaking through jungle. The singing continued, accompanying the movements of her body, rising and falling in pitch as she stooped to make a mark with a long wand, tipped with a brush. There were words to her song. Occasionally I could detect a rhyme but the words themselves were strange to me: perhaps a dialect. I noticed, propped against the wall, a mirror; an unframed rectangle of glass that might have come from a barber's shop. Maria Pia was observing her movements in its reflection, and it seemed she was transcribing some essence of them onto the canvas on the floor. Then I saw there was a second reflection. Someone was sitting in the corner behind the door I'd just opened: it was Matteo; he was wearing a bathrobe. The scene was one of domesticity, almost.

Catching sight of me, he seemed at pains to prevent the spell being broken. He half whispered, 'Maria Pia needs to be like this, to make her paintings. It's a psychic state, a trance if you like.'

I was in no mood to be hushed; I felt suddenly angry at being used for their games. I was the Visigoths entering Rome, I was Attila before Vienna, I was the Rolling Stones on the road. The paints that Maria Pia was using stood in a cluster of open pots, just off the canvas. I took a swing at them with my foot. I was evidently not properly connected up with the physical world, because only one went over, but it was enough. Maria Pia stopped and looked, seeing me for the first time.

'How much juice did you put in your drinks?' I barked.

'Juice? It wasn't—'

'LSD, I mean. You know what I'm talking about.'

Matteo looked uncomfortable but prepared to talk me down. He was going to be a trickcyclist. This was psychodrama.

'It's not so simple. What is a lot? The quantities are always very small. The effects vary according to the individual —'

'Stop being a fucking Jesuit. You've done this plenty of times before. A lot or a little? That's all I'm asking…'

'Perhaps a significant amount – but it's not guesswork, you understand. This is a controlled situation…'

Maria Pia was staring at me, her face welling like a bruise. The pool of paint spreading on the floor shimmered a rainbow of vibrating colours. I wanted to slap her, I wanted to pull her down into the ooze. I was the Visigoths, I was Attila etc. etc. A fly was buzzing in the light shade. My guardian, it was sending me a message: something significant. I veered out of the room, and headed downstairs, where I could hear voices. I was still thirsty.

On the first floor was a sitting-room. It had a latter-day elegance: moulded ceiling; a fireplace from the Risorgimento; gilded mirror over. There was a record player in the middle of the floor, surrounded by a midden of LPs. Nothing was playing, but a couple of girls were dancing barefoot. One was Laura. On a beanbag in the corner, Casanova lay like a satrap, his hand absently cradling the breast of a girl who looked to be asleep.

I went up to Laura, who drew me into a strange three-way huddle with the other girl, her dance partner.

'Adam, Adam, listen, I need to tell you…' Her voice was a confidential whisper. She looked over her shoulder into the corner, and giggled. 'No, just listen, will you…' Her voice became school-marmish.

'I am listening,' I said, waiting. She giggled again.

'It's Casanova. He says he wants me. He says it's his *droit du seigneur…*'

'What are you talking about? The guy's a creep.'

'I wanna get laid. You have…' Her mouth had a lascivious twist. She laughed, then a thought crossed her mind like cloud shadow through a sunlit vale. 'Creep. You're right. Big creep. But then he *is* Casanova. Does it count as creepy if that's who you are?'

'What do you mean "if that's who you are"? He's just a jerk in Fauntleroy bags.'

'No, no he *is* Casanova, he is really.' She looked at me wide-eyed, desperate that I should believe her. 'You are Casanova, you are, aren't you?' she said, turning round to address the reclining satyr on his gingham throne.

'A descendant, yes,' Casanova nodded sententiously.

'You see,' said Laura, vindicated. 'It's like destiny. He fucks, fucks, fucks, and fucks again. He fucks 'em all. He fucked Maria Pia. That's when all the trouble started, with Danny —'

'What trouble? Danny, where is he?'

Laura looked troubled. 'He got really angry. He was with Maria Pia. He thought he was. Then he found… He just started lashing out at everyone, raging…'

'The guy was freakin' everyone out,' Casanova spoke up from the corner. 'We had to put him in the cooler. For his own sake. Bad trip!'

'Where is he? What have you done with him?' I looked Casanova in the eye with murder in my heart. 'Where's my fucking mate?'

'Hey cool, man. It's all cool. He's just downstairs, in the bathroom…'

I didn't stop to hear any more. I was the man in the poncho. I had a town to clean up. I turned to go out of the door.

'Casanova. He died of pox. That was his destiny. Stay away from him,' I said to Laura over my shoulder as I went.

9.

I should have asked where the bathroom was, because, blundering through various rooms, I got contradictory directions. The group of players and party-goers were enjoying diverse forms of altered consciousness. Some were asleep, or as near comatose as makes no difference. Some were inhabiting other bodies, and too preoccupied by their mutual explorations to deal with my enquiry. Some, quite a number, were inclined towards blissfully inane circumlocutions that, at another time, might have gathered me into their bubble of omni-love, but now caused annoyance.

'The bathroom, man? That's a B-I-G-G question...big like the whole universe...like it's t-h-i-s big (indicating with finger and thumb a millimetre apart)...or maybe...hey, man, don't go, this is like really major...'

I guided myself by wrong turnings, by déjà vu, and when I grew warmer, by sound, because I became aware of a feral moaning, muffled but audible, rising and falling in a regular rhythm like a mechanism being cranked. It came from behind a half-glazed door. The room it guarded was dark within. I rattled the door. It was locked. I called out for Danny who was, I presumed, making the noise, even though the sound of it was scarcely human. There was no answer, simply the continued moaning or howling; it was both at different times. Far from Danny having been locked in the 'cooler', the opposite had occurred. He had locked himself in. There was no telling what he would do in there, I thought, once his vocal chords gave out.

I had always wanted to kick in a door. For the past half hour I had wanted to kick most things. Here was a legitimate reason and I was going to take advantage of it. I stood back and stomped my foot against the lock. It didn't give. Nothing much happened except for the sharp pain in my heel.

'Hey cool, hombre!' I turned and found Actaeon beside me. He was dressed in a sort of nightshirt. Just behind him stood Daisy. They looked as if they had just been roused from slumber.

'Danny – my friend Danny – is in there. He doesn't sound in good shape. I need to get in,' I said, giving my voice the urgency of the Lone Ranger announcing a plan.

'You should be very careful, he's crazy. He bit Casanova. Maybe you should just leave him.' I found the biting news heartening evidence of rationality, but the noise continued. More than anything, I wanted it to stop.

'No, I need to get in,' I said, preparing to take another kick.

'Hey no, easy, man. Just wait a second...' Actaeon made a pacifying gesture, and disappeared into an adjoining room.

Daisy and I stood where we were, awkwardly saying nothing.

A moment later he came back holding a knife. I felt a prickle of cold sweat: what if he'd slipped into his parallel identity as 'the huntsman'? However it was just a kitchen knife. The door proved to be one with a blind screw to operate the lock from the other side, for just such eventualities as this: to provide access when the facilities are occupied by a lunatic.

He worked the catch, and we inched open the door. The bathroom was not much more than a corridor with a basin and toilet; a pail and mop were stationed behind the door. It ended in a window that took up nearly the full width of the room. There was light enough from the hallway to detect a figure, a silhouette, crouching on the sill of the open window. I could tell it was Danny from the shape of his mop of hair, but he was facing outwards. He didn't see us. He was rocking on his haunches, making his noise, like a dog baying at the moon, except there was none; instead only the sparse firmament of lights belonging to insomniacs in the surrounding apartment blocks.

'Hey, Danny, it's time to go...' I said in a voice that could have been designed to calm a ferocious beast.

He turned his head, as if weary, but continued making the noise.

'That's enough of that, Danny. Let's split...' I began to move forward, towards him.

'Filth! The filth in here!' His eyes were darting all over the place.

'C'mon, it's time to go,' I said, inching forwards.

'I'm ready,' he said, smiling as if recognising a secret command that he had been waiting to hear. 'I've learnt to fly. I've been taking in the knowledge.' He lowered his voice confidentially. 'They don't know how. Filth doesn't fly – but flies like filth.' He laughed at his quip.

41

Then he turned away. Before I could react, he disappeared through the window. There was an echoing whump! – as he hit concrete – followed by a clatter of bins. I felt sick. I could hear voices cursing, coming from the flats just over the back wall. In the search for the bathroom, I'd become disoriented: I had no idea what storey we were on. Fearing the worst, I rushed to the window and stared down into a pool of darkness. I couldn't make out Danny, but at least I could tell this was the first floor and no higher. Perhaps it wasn't a fatal drop, but then again – the bins! If they were down another level, a basement maybe? No further sounds were to be heard; that was worrying.

'Danny, Danny, you crazy idiot! Are you OK?' The only answer came from across the way.

'Madonna! Four in the morning! That fucking commune – I'm getting the police. Anna, call the police. Tell 'em there's druggies. Tell 'em there's an orgy goin' on...'

'You tell 'em, why don'tcha?' came a second voice, more annoyed, it seemed, by this proposed escalation than by the clamour caused by us. 'The police are going to love you for getting them out – yeah, why not call our good friends, the pigs? They'll thank you! An' wanna poke around in our business, while they're at it. God give me strength, get back inside...'

While this exchange was going on, I tried my best to listen for signs of life down below.

'Danny, are you OK?' I strained my ears, but all I could hear were the voices opposite, still bickering. I called down, 'Stay put, I'm coming.' As I turned to go out of the bathroom, I barged into the mop and bucket, adding more racket to the night air. On the stairs I met Actaeon going the other way.

'Danny, he's knocked himself out...' He had an air of concern.

'Jesus, he's not dead?'

'No, no, he's making a noise, like he's, er,' he paused to select his word, 'awaking... I'm going to get Matteo. He's a doctor, sort of...'

I hurried past him. Getting Matteo, the original cause of all this, would be like asking a pyromaniac to put out a fire. I blundered on.

Outside, in the lee of the house, it was pitch black. I looked up to the bathroom window, to try and work out where Danny should be. In looking up, I lost balance and fell over the same bins he'd already disturbed. Their clatter made a mocking echo off the walls and concrete. I lay on the ground clutching the knee I had cracked, waiting for the pain to drain away. Beside me I heard sounds, a scuffling and a snorting, as if I were in the lair of some beast.

'Danny?'

The presence beside me propelled itself out of the cavernous space, disturbing another bin in the process.

'Danny? Wait on, Danny!'

Light from the bathroom painted a distorted rectangle across the yard. Flushed from cover among the trash cans and rubbish, a figure passed through it. The silhouette of Danny's mop confirmed his identity. His lopsided gait betold the painful impact of his fall; he could have been a Yeti.

A voice called down from above: Daisy's. 'Adam, what's happening?' That's the question, I thought. What *is* happening – to us all?

10.

I needed to catch up with Danny, my mate, my old roomie.

'Hey, Danny, wait on. Let's go back home...'

He didn't falter. I heard his footsteps echoing in the passage onto the street. I made to follow but my leg wouldn't work. I dragged it to the doorway. The outer door was ajar – left open by him as he went out. I stepped into the roadway, with a sense of relief to be out of the house. Thankfully I was starting to receive the world on a normal waveband; the crack on the knee had cleared my head. The scattered street-lights showed as clear points: no rainbows, no mergings, no dazzle. I looked both ways, hoping to catch sight of Danny. Panic set in until I spotted him passing a lamp-post, slipping through its pool of light like a spectre.

He had made some ground and was perhaps a hundred yards down the road. Although he was stockily built, Danny was a good athlete. I set off after him, but found it impossible to close the distance between us. My leg hurt. It had gone weak. I was obliged to limp in a mimicry of his listing stride. I settled for tailing him through the darkened streets, like his displaced shadow. I sometimes lost sight of him, and was obliged to stop and listen. My ears became those of a hunter, acutely tuned to detecting the uneven rhythm of his steps on the pavement. He moved with tireless purpose, ungainly but steady – going where? I didn't recognise the streets we took, apart from knowing we weren't heading back into the city, and, therefore, weren't bound for home. Thanks to my friend the fly, my dosage of Matteo's cocktail had been less than Danny's. His trip was still happening. It had become a fugue, an end in itself. I told myself I had to keep tabs on him; I needed to wait for the effects to wear off.

Dogged and bent on my resolve, I shambled on, all sense of time lost; the only thing that existed for me was this journey through strange undifferentiated places. At a certain point, the hitherto deserted roads discharged stinking eruptions in the form of trucks, laden and ponderous, setting out to provision the day ahead. Sometimes our unforeseen presence would spook their drivers and they would exorcise us with a long jarring

note on the klaxon. Indigo rinsed from the night sky. The morning star hung in the pure ether of a day in waiting, defying the sun to erase its pinpoint.

~ o ~

Danny's pace didn't slacken; and so we forged on, as if we were climbers roped together. We marched through the marginal fringes of the city, a territory of dumps, and yards, and odd isolated houses, the last outposts of conurbia. There was more traffic now, its proximity deafening. The gathering hubbub of the morning had no use for us in its pageant of purposive actions; it cast us as a pair of hobos, the objects of suspicious glances, even gestures of hostility or derision. Indeed, we did have a ragged look about us, and the telltale trudge of the desperate in our stride. Also, I had one foot unaccountably painted red, a warning to all I might encounter.

Towards midday, I became desperate for water. Every dip in the road before me contained a shimmering pool whose shores forever receded. I spotted a filling station in the distance: a flat-roofed bunker cowering beneath the confident yellow canopy of *SAGIT*, the fire-spewing lion.

The road was straight for as far as the eye could see. It was a featureless section of three-lane highway. Infrequent trucks could be seen approaching in the far distance, giving notice to stiffen against a buffeting from their slipstreams. I decided it was safe to dodge into the kiosk to get water, without losing touch with Danny.

There was an elderly lank-haired woman behind the counter, fanning herself with a magazine. It was dingy indoors, and perhaps her eyesight was poor. In any case, the incongruity of my presence caused her no pause. Her greeting as I entered – 'Fine day for a lovely walk' – was quite without irony.

She sold me a bottle of water from the crate behind her, but the transaction got bogged down in the search for change. There was a failure of the monetary system in the country. Coinage had all but disappeared from circulation, a conspiracy of the politicians and bigwig industrialists to ramp prices, ran one rumour. Another had it that there were now so many killings in Italy – variously ascribed to the mafia and to far-left extremists – that all

46

the coins were getting used up: weighting the eyes of the dead. Whatever the theory, the missing coinage was a mysterious but tedious reality.

She rejected my suggestion that she keep the difference, and instead rooted around behind her for something to offer in kind. Eventually, I accepted a couple of tomatoes, a deal that left both parties satisfied.

When I re-emerged, there was no sign of Danny. Half running, weighed down by the bottle, and juggling the tomatoes, I set off up the road as best I could. Maybe there was a dip in the terrain, and I would see him climbing out the other side? However there was nothing. I covered easily half a mile, which I judged to be more ground than he could have travelled in the time; then I retraced my steps part of the way, but there was still no sign. I sat and took a long pull on the water, trying to gather my thoughts. I found I had very few, apart from being tired and thirsty. I could hear birdsong. I could hear the wind humming in the power lines beside the road.

I am not sure how much time passed. As I sat savouring the taste of the water, I was aware of a moped approaching from the opposite direction. I could see it was ridden by a youth, perhaps thirteen or fourteen years old. Instead of passing me, he stopped, the motor still running.

'We've got your friend,' he said, not meeting my eye as he spoke.

'Where is he?' I asked, presuming he was referring to Danny, but wondering how he knew he had anything to do with me. The kid didn't answer. He held out his hand and gave a shrug. He was a young chancer. For a moment, I thought he was trying to say they had kidnapped him.

'Where is he?' I repeated, standing up and approaching the moped. I must have looked a desperate type. He thought better of holding out for his fee. He made a gesture with his head, indicating back up the road.

'I wanna see him. Take me there.'

He vacated the seat of the moped, so that I could mount it to ride tandem behind him. The machine did a struggling U-turn, and we set off up the road. Some way further on was a farm track, flanked by a ditch. It led to a quadrangle of buildings, partly hidden by a stand of cypresses.

We stopped where the track joined the main road. I saw Danny. He was lying on his back in the ditch. His head rested beside the water collected in the bottom; his feet were angled up the slope, pointing skywards. There was another kid, a bit younger than the first, wearing shorts. He was sitting watching Danny, like a shepherd boy on guard.

'Hey, Danny, it's Adam. Hey, man, are you OK?' He didn't move or answer.

With some assistance from the elder boy, I heaved him out of the ditch and got him sitting on the bank. I offered him the remains of my water, which he drank but still made no sign of recognising me. I sat beside him on the ground, waiting for him to revive and snap out of his passivity. The boys stood by, watching to see how this strange business would go.

'Danny, we can't stay here. We need to move. We can get some more water, then we can try and get back to town.' I thought I could detect signs of his hearing what I was saying. I stood up, and hauled on his arm. Thankfully, he offered no resistance, but got to his feet.

'C'mon, let's get going. Let's walk.' I set off, then turned; to my relief I saw he was following me. 'C'mon, let's go.' I resumed walking. The elder boy held out his hand as I passed him, a last attempt to make some profit from the episode. I proffered the two tomatoes, reasoning that they had the status of currency. However the offer was declined. His look of pity suggested he didn't share my thinking.

~ o ~

We retraced our journey, in inverse fashion to the way we had accomplished it: I led; he followed, at a distance of twenty yards, his eyes fixed on his feet, yet never falling back or failing to mirror my changes in direction. I was weary, and so must he have been. I would have dearly loved a lift, but our dishevelled appearance made the hope unlikely.

Yet, to my surprise, we did get one ride: in a trailer hitched to a filthy tractor that blasted mud from its wheels. We sheltered in the shadow of the trailer's boarding, among dirty sacks, sharing the space with the farmer's deranged mutt. By the time we reached the peripheries of the city once more, we had undergone a transformation into a rankly untouchable sub-species. We rode the bus to our area of town, attracting looks of disgust from fellow passengers, in their Sunday best, heading for the swanky streets to join in the *passeggiata*.

I looked across at Danny, filthy and dishevelled and broken – I realised as much even then. In a way, I was looking at my own reflection: I was as filthy and stinking as he was; we both now dwelt in the wilderness of estrangement from Love. The thought returned to me: 'What is happening – to us, all of us?'

11.

We got back to our place. There was no sign of Daisy. As well, perhaps, that she did not witness our sub-human incarnations.

Danny's demeanour remained the same as it had been since I had found him. On my prompting he cleaned up. Though mute and inert, he was thankfully biddable.

He was due at work that evening. I was dubious whether he could do his shift, but if he didn't show, he would be fired. When the time came, I took him to the restaurant where he washed dishes. I found Marco, Danny's fellow *plongeur*, the guy with the rat. I didn't quite know how to explain his predicament, but Marco, seeing Danny's unfocused eyes, made gestures miming pulling on a joint and shook his head.

'Too much partying, big guy,' he said in English, wagging his index finger under Danny's nose.

'You know how it is, Marco, the weekend scene,' I said, thankful that he had constructed this explanation for himself. He took Danny by the arm. Perhaps he saw a new challenge for his training abilities: one to supersede the rat project.

That night Danny came back with Annalisa, the waitress. Our flat was on the rooftop of a pensione. I arranged for him to bed down there, where I and the others could keep an eye on him.

Annalisa was an unmarried mother, holding down two jobs. As a good-looking young woman, naturally vivacious, regular offers to date came her way but she had little time or appetite for it. The 'romance' with the client had not blossomed.

I asked how Danny had been. He had got through his shift. It was OK, she assured me, whilst flashing a look that said she thought it my fault that he had come to this pass.

In the days that followed, Danny remained much the same. Daisy returned, but was unforthcoming about anything to do with the séance, beyond establishing that Danny had been found, and dropping downstairs to spend some time with him. She was not willing to be drawn about Actaeon – nor I, for that matter, about Agata. That seemed to be how the open couple thing worked.

I sought out Laura. I needed someone to consult. She seemed unaffected by the LSD experience. I wanted to ask about Casanova but we left the subject unbroached; I took it she was in no hurry to recount the episode's denouement. It was Danny and his altered state that I needed to talk about. I described the fugue, and the way he had been ever since.

'He's catatonic,' Laura concluded.

'He's what?'

'Like a schizo.'

'Not literally, surely? Not medically speaking? Danny's not bonkers…'

'He's acting "bonkers", isn't he? You know what they say, if it walks like a dick,' she giggled, 'like a duck, I mean…'

'It's no joking matter…'

'Sorry, Freudian slip.'

'Having flashbacks, are we?' I regretted the waspish tone as soon as I had spoken. It was an overspill from the tension in the flat; Daisy was the one I wanted to spite. Even so, I was prey to a prurient curiosity whether Laura did 'get laid'.

'Aren't we supposed to be talking about Danny?' An edge crept into Laura's voice too. She was ready for the fight – our fight – one that intermittently flared between us since *that* time: a drunken night when we had fallen into bed. There persisted a temptation to taunt the other with what might have been; to dangle an invitation to go in search of lost threads. It seemed, wherever you looked, the accursed séance had shaken loose our moorings.

'Quite right – it *is* Danny we need to talk about. We *are* talking about him. You were saying he's catatonic…'

'All I mean is that he's acting as if something is really wrong, clinically wrong. Schizophrenia, what is that? A person splits himself, because he experiences conflicting realities. R. D. Laing – "The Divided Self" – it's all in there.'

'I don't see how that relates to Danny – it's a whole lot simpler, isn't it? He got hit with a Matteo-style Mickey Finn that he wasn't bargaining for; a whole lot more than I did, incidentally, and maybe you? Who the hell knows what Dr Mengele was up to there? And wham! He's into a bum trip.'

'All that's true, but Danny was fixated by Maria Pia. He's been building up to the séance – she's been building him up to it. He thinks the moment's come: he's in love and – let's face it – he is a child in that respect. He thinks they're forever: it's the *Sound of Music* with fucking – then, guess what? – he finds Maria Pia with someone else; he can't deal with it…'

'What did happen there, actually?'

'Of course, you were otherwise occupied, I recall…' It was Laura's turn to be waspish.

'Let's just talk about Danny – d'you know what went on?'

'Well, as far as I can gather, he lost Maria Pia and went around looking for her. I know that because he asked me where she was. I saw him wandering around, but he was quite happy at that stage, well you know – spaced and happy in the "hey, man, far out" kind of way. Then, he found her and she was screwing someone. Then he really started: raving, shouting. He actually bit—'

'Yes, I know, he got a piece of Casanova. Was it him Maria Pia was balling?'

'Maybe,' said Laura, colouring a little. I felt a cheap pleasure at her discomfort. 'Anyway,' she continued, 'he quietened after a time, and people gave him some space, then he locked himself in the bathroom.'

'So you think that's flipped him, for good, is that it?'

'It's conceivable, isn't it?'

'Conceivable, yes.'

We fell silent, each considering what that possibility held out: what it meant for Danny, and what it required of us. Neither of us wanted to explore the implications right there. After a while, to usher out the topic, I said, 'We'll have to give him time, and see if he snaps out of it.'

'He probably will,' said Laura firmly, ending further speculation.

~ o ~

Danny did show signs of improvement, even if he did not exactly 'snap out of it'. He began to react, when addressed, with a smile – a smile that was broad and frank, and wrapped around a fog of puzzlement. Though, all things considered, this was a welcome development, it was heartbreaking if you dwelt on it, which I preferred not to. The next breakthrough was that he started speaking again. His utterances were formulaic: 'billiant', and 'luvely job' were two standbys. I surmised that he had dredged these up to carry him through his shifts at work. If he could meet all requests with a smile and a 'luvely job', everyone was happy. He took himself to work now, which I was glad of, and Annalisa continued to see him home.

The final great leap forward was that he began playing the guitar again, spontaneously, and rather well. Not only that, but from somewhere he discovered a voice. Previously he had been an aspiring Bream, sticking with classical repertoire, but in his renascent musical incarnation he crossed over: into folk ballads. He soon had an affecting rendition of 'Streets of London'. This never failed to bring our fugue back to my memory, and perhaps also to his. Actually, I wondered whether, as far as he was concerned at least, the fugue still continued; the song was perhaps his testimony, his correspondent's despatches. In a way you might have said that he had reacquired a sufficient complement of social graces: a smile for all seasons; a couple of handy phrases and an admirable turn on the guitar. Such is a man.

12.

Laura continued to frequent Maria Pia. I believe she took LSD on a few more occasions, with no bad effects as far as I could see, but from what she said, with diminishing pleasure. The sense of oneness, the extraordinary delight in the *thing-ness* of things, these became rare fruit. Perhaps a fear of what had happened to Danny had set in, and prevented the experience from flowing.

She taxed Maria Pia with her treatment of Danny. Maria Pia would only say that he was not in her destiny. She had been 'nice' to him, but he was like a puppy, exuberant in his affection, and had made her feel a responsibility that was not in her destiny either. She elaborated: she was a free spirit, an artist; she could not belong to anyone exclusively or have anyone depend on her; she had many lovers, as many as she pleased; it was in her destiny to 'grow' in this way. Such was Laura's précis. When she recounted it, I could hear Maria Pia's disdain in my head. More succinctly, Danny was a pet she had grown tired of and left by the road, to fend, or not.

~ o ~

Perhaps six weeks after the séance, I met Agata. I found her one day in the street, waiting for me after a drawing class. We went to Rocco's Counter and sat on stools in the window, with our portions of Polpetti. It was a spiteful March day; people were in winter coats. She asked after Danny and I reported the news. She seemed more genuinely concerned for him than her sister, whose demeanour at class these days was decidedly cool towards me.

Agata was planning to move out of the house. She was looking for a place. It seemed to be one of those times when settled arrangements were dissolving. Our group was dispersing too: Daisy would be gone soon, back to England. Danny's room-mate, Robin, was also about to return. I considered whether his room might serve her needs. I liked Agata. If I could help her out, it would be good.

I began to talk about Danny. She would be better company for him than some random new face. I was saying something pompous, along the lines that his immaturity had been responsible for Danny's reaction, when he found Maria Pia with someone else.

'I don't see that,' she said. 'I think he is basically a strong person, but what he saw would really shock anyone. He thought Maria Pia felt something for him but when he found her—'

'With Casanova? But you might have guessed that those two had history...'

'Casanova?' She looked puzzled. 'Is that what you think? No, no, it wasn't Casanova... No... She paused, then, in a flat voice, said, 'It was Matteo.'

I stopped chewing mid-mouthful – dumbfounded: nothing to say for long seconds, whilst things began falling into place. Of course, I had sensed the particular closeness – and the complicity – between brother and sister; but this was something I had never dreamt of. I stared through the window, all my recollections and impressions of Maria Pia slowly marinading in this new understanding. I saw now what Agata meant. Discovering them – in the weird circumstances of the *séance* – certainly qualified as traumatic. I swallowed, not sure how to ask what I wanted to know.

'That's a lot to take in,' I began. 'Have they...has *this* been happening for a long time? I mean, are we talking just the one occasion – the séance – or is it...is it regular?'

'It happens,' she said, visibly uncomfortable at the prospect of being quizzed. 'Maria Pia is...experimental...and Matteo has certain beliefs, well they both do...'

'Beliefs?'

'They don't consider there should be barriers – taboos, that sort of thing – in the way of a person expressing their nature. Or their "destiny", as Maria would say. They think we are all brought up with hang-ups, social conditioning, all that stuff, and we've got to free ourselves. That's where LSD comes in. Matteo thinks it's the truth drug...'

'And, he's happy to drag anyone he likes into his social experiment?'

'If you like – yes.'

'And Danny, he's a guinea pig? Just a test in their lab? One that went wrong – their Frankenstein – but so what? Nothing can stand in the way of personal growth, can it? Onwards and upwards – doing any damn thing you like.'

'Matteo is really sorry about Danny, really…but he thinks finding out about yourself, about your real nature is painful quite often. He thinks Danny is kind of stuck. He would like to help him…'

'Another go with LSD?…and some psycho-quackery? I think he'd be better off without help of that sort.'

'I don't blame you for thinking that way. I agree, I think.'

'What about you? You said you're moving out?' Then it struck me: what was true of Maria Pia, could it also be true of Agata?

'It's difficult for me. We were all brought up in that house. We only had ourselves, really. We were left with our grandparents…but I don't agree with them, Maria and Matteo. I don't agree with what they're doing. Everything's so intense… I have to get away and leave them to their crazy stuff…'

I could hear determination in her voice. To be part of the *ménage* or left out of it: neither were comfortable options.

'So unconstrained freedom – truth *uber alles* – you're not convinced of the programme?' A thought surfaced: a few months ago, I might have signed up to the idea myself, but those convictions had since crumbled.

'I think it's good to have some things that hold you back. That's my freedom, anyway: I choose to hold onto some rules; that's how I know who I am…is that a stupid compromise?'

'No. You've found that out for yourself. Matteo's experiment has worked for you, in that way, at least.'

We made a date. There was open-air ballroom dancing coming up on Sunday afternoons. Agata was confident she could teach me.

~ o ~

It was some months after this conversation, in the summer, that Danny announced he was engaged to Annalisa.

He had been going round to her place regularly for some time, her place being the apartment she shared with her parents and her daughter. I had also seen them out and about, the two of them with the little girl, looking like a regular family. Perhaps that was it, those mealtimes with the family gathered around the table: they were the familiar landscape of Danny's youth; they had restored him, or most of him, at any rate. Perhaps too, having someone who mattered, to whom you mattered, with whom you stood on solid ground – that was what it took to have the necessary sense of yourself. Otherwise what was there? Falling. That was all.

The wedding was to be at the beginning of September, the second anniversary of his arrival in the city. I was to be best man.

A full length novel, soon to be released from this author: —

Beauty on the Streets

A love affair, a country on the brink of revolution...

Rome, 1969. Davey Marks has fallen in love – twice. Once with the vibrant and turbulent place that is Italy, and secondly with Carol, a beautiful young woman determined to live recklessly.

A year since protesters in Prague faced tanks in the streets and revolutionary uprisings shook Paris, Italy is rocked by strikes and demonstrations; it is exhilarating – and dangerous. Revolution seems possible, even inevitable. There are violent clashes with the authorities, and Davey and his activist friends are forced into hiding.

As political tensions abate, everything is left upside down. Carol has been drawn into the orbit of Sabetta, an underworld figure. Davey is obliged to negotiate a menacing world of political action, street violence and criminality. With sinister forces at work, who will pay the ultimate price?

Beauty on the Streets is the first volume in an epic coming-of-age story. It is a tale of love — compulsive and destructive — played out against a backdrop of political unrest.

Also awaiting release, the sequel to 'Beauty on the Streets': —

On Wings of Lead

Beauty on the Streets

(Sample)

'The revolutionary movement can be nothing less than the struggle of the proletariat for the actual domination and deliberate transformation of all aspects of social life – beginning with the management of production and work by the workers themselves, directly deciding everything.' (Guy Debord)

1.

To slide into its cool waters became my deepest wish as soon as we found ourselves driving beside the lake. It might even have been the very lake we'd been looking for — the one that Costa half remembered and we'd stopped believing in. It was sizeable, perhaps a half mile across, fringed with trees and bamboo. At frequent intervals there were places where cars could pull in and the shore-line was indented with small bays, some of which had a suggestion of beach. The water was placid and lapped an invitation against the cordon of greenery holding back the exhausted dust of the roadside. The scene was completed by a staffage of fishermen, occupying shaded spots on the water's edge or lolling in small boats. The temperature was still fierce — in the nineties.

We rummaged in our bags, donned swimming suits and went down to the shoreline where the others were already gathered. They'd found a sort of miniature cove just beyond the *albergo* we'd chanced on, and where we'd decided to stay the night ('motion carried unanimously', ruled Massimo). It was screened by a couple of tamarinds and more bamboo. Bare earth gave way to coarse sand at the water's margin. The relief of being released from the broiling monotony of the road turned us into excitable children. We horsed around in the shallows, played piggy-in-the-middle with a buoy that had become detached and stranded in 'our bay'. This side of the lake faced west, and the rays of the sinking sun drenched us when we came out of the water. We sat down on the meagre beach to dry off in the warmth bleeding from the land. It was a moment, perhaps, that you remember all your life.

~ o ~

Massimo and Costa were talking – again – about what went wrong in Paris, and how it didn't need to happen that way.

'I might go back in – for a proper swim.' Carol's voice seemed to come to me on the breeze. Now I could feel her breath in my ear. 'You can fuck me when I come out, if you like.' She was gone, striding purposefully into the water. I was left wondering whether she intended an *al fresco* tryst, or something safer and more conjugal back in the room. She was swimming now, cleaving the still surface; her regular breaststroke caused a bow-wave to spread a surprising distance either side of her progress.

'Sporty.' Paolo commented. I believed he was thinking how easily things could have worked out differently: he and Carol sharing the double room, and me bunking in with Massimo. I wondered as I often did – was life wholly shaped by accidents? Or did whatever was due to happen force its way, no matter what, up through the shambolic tangle of randomness?

Mary picked up Paolo's observation. 'Sporty? Going for a swim? That's what guys say, isn't it? If a woman does something aside from dancing, shopping, or sex?'

'Just saying...' said Paolo, looking towards Costa, hoping, perhaps, that he would rein in 'his woman'; a laughable notion if you knew Mary. In Rome hers had been a powerful voice in the secretly organised seminar we'd attended, in the apartment of one Roberto who was actually there: Paris: 1968; the revolution that happened, so nearly happened until it faltered – but wasn't over yet.

Mary and Paolo often grated on each other. As she saw it, her days of deference to men were over. She had walked out on Ivo, a 'bourgeois' (as she now referred to him), whose infidelities had finally exasperated her; divorce was outlawed in Italy so quitting a marriage was a brave step. Mary decided to cut short the conversation. Looking at Costa she said, 'Let's get going; we need to smarten up for dinner, I guess.' The two of them picked themselves up and dusted off the gritty sand. It was a general signal.

'Man, am I hungry!' I heard Massimo saying. When I looked, he was trotting away to catch up Paolo who was already halfway back to the terrace.

I settled back to daydream, grateful for an empty moment. When I looked up, Carol was floating well out from the shore. The sky was turning pink; the wavering reflections on the surface of the lake were slick and glossy in the fading light. The only sounds came from the kitchen of the rest house: the occasional clunk of a pan being set down. I looked at Carol, wondering when she would turn for the shore.

We'd met by chance. One morning, I opened the grand nail-studded door to Roberto's stairway and found her the other side of it, in the street. She was lost. I invited her in, and she stayed. Carol was, I now believed in a superstitious sort of way, 'my luck'; her unsolicited appearance was a sign that other things I hoped for could also come to pass. So, here we were, in a 'matrimonial bedroom' — another omen, if you liked to see it that way — with a wash basin in the corner.

I saw she was making no movements; she seemed to be floating face down. At that distance it was difficult to see whether she was taking breaths; she barely projected above the surface. Some quality of her stillness made me grow uneasy. She appeared quite lifeless. After the heat of the journey, I wondered, had the cold shock of the water caused her to pass out?

2.

It had been that kind of scene in Rome: people came, stayed a while, then went. It is possible that Roberto knew them but I believe the majority had come because they could sense something was in the air.

The apartment was a shabby, spacious and largely empty collection of high-ceilinged rooms; original aristocratic mouldings were mocked by a cacophony of loud wallpapers. I think the gathering, chaotic though it seemed, took exactly the form Roberto had in mind. It developed a constantly shifting periphery. People dropped in and out; pressed forward like spectators at a sideshow to hear the speakers, and then drifted away. Others settled themselves around the floor of the onetime formal drawing room, sprawling out as if it were Sunday in the park.

'This is a moment of great historical significance,' Roberto was fond of saying. 'The proletarian struggle is not to be conducted on our behalf by experts, by politicos, by careerists, by the Communist Party, the Socialist Party, the Radical Party or any other party... No – the struggle is *us*; it takes place wherever we gather.'

The 'happening' at Roberto's never paused; even in the small hours conversations were taking place and earlier arguments being re-run. It spawned a complex social texture that expanded to occupy all the rooms and spaces in the commodious apartment. It was a party fuelled by wine and weed; it was a laboratory where ideas were launched, spoken out loud into a charged atmosphere of expectant intoxication; it was an encampment where people ate and slept irrespective of time of day. There was music: guitar players pulling in a circle of listeners or teaching chords to other players. There was dancing, a lot of dancing; there was semi-nakedness; there was nakedness; and there was a lot of sex, not all enacted in obscure corners or sleeping bags.

Carol had an unobtrusive quality that made her easy to overlook. She wore baggy outfits – loons, kaftan and flip-flops – and these shrouded the otherwise slightness of her build. On the day she turned up by accident, she stayed to listen for an hour or so. I watched her whenever I thought she wouldn't notice. Something about her took me a time to absorb: another age would have instantly declared her 'a beauty'. When she released her pony tail her blond hair fell into ringlets; her cheeks had the perpetual flush of a healthy-complexioned farm girl; exotic in this country of tanned features.

When she got up to leave, that first time, I found myself following her into the street.

'So, what did you make of it all?'

She shrugged but sat down on the pavement and began compiling a roll-up; she carried the makings – she carried everything – in a carpet bag slung from her shoulder.

I sat beside her as she made up a second cigarette for me; the fact that she had worked out that I smoked produced a kind of intimacy. We talked about the usual things, where we came from, where we were going. The second question is the one I always found unsettling: the future seemed both infinite and empty; it had little in common with the past, with what I knew.

In Roberto's place an over-mantle mirror remained in what had once been a dining room: history's spy glass. It would constantly surprise me with a sight of myself; pale-skinned despite the hours of exposure waiting for lifts by roadsides; awkward shouldered among the bronzed, athletically formed figures milling around me.

At those times I would stare back at myself – at *me* – considering whether I was nearer or further from my desire to appear solid; a somebody you could put a name to. At home I was Dave to most – but David to my father and his generation; here, I am Davey. Three people seeking to become one. Davey Marks...the man: that would be enough if I knew the constituent parts. As it is, I held onto a secret knowledge of myself, of something inside that the world would come to know...in time.

I had left on bad terms; a runaway. 'David, you will not go, d'you hear! You will not waste your time, your future gallivanting around bloody Italy...' My father had journeyed the length of Italy with the Eighth Army; the country had been sufficiently explored by our family, in his view.

Carol was sketchy in divulging her own origins. I learned her parents were separated. She lived with her mother and stepfather but owned up to spending little time with them now that she was at university. This summer she was travelling, had come to Rome but was bored with sightseeing. A guy she had been travelling with – I inferred he had been less than a boyfriend but more than a companion – had left to go to Greece. Carol was on the point of moving on herself.

'When things are played out there's no point hanging around waiting for them to get duller. You're a long time dead...' This last phrase was one Carol frequently reverted to.

As if to demonstrate her philosophy she got up abruptly and made to leave, arranging the bag across her shoulder, putting back her tobacco and papers.

'You're welcome to come back. Roberto's seminar (Roberto's preferred description for the comings and goings in his apartment) is on all the time. Anyone who's interested is welcome, anyone who's going to take a hand...'

'The revolution?' Carol said the word with a sceptical smile, of course.

'Who knows? Things are happening, that's all I know. I'm for pitching in; you're a long time...'

'...dead? That's my line you stole there.' Carol was mistress of the direct look; her eyes were a translucent grey, like moonstones; they drew you into their orbit. Personally, I'm inclined to avoid looking people directly in the eye until I think I have them worked out. Being held in her gaze created an unease that she was fully aware of: Carol liked to tease. We had joked a lot – but on this occasion I detected a chill in her voice. It was absurd but it felt as if I had trespassed by borrowing her stock phrase.

'Do you reckon you'll be back?' I asked. She was walking away now. I hoped to hear her say, Sure! See you tomorrow. She merely looked back and gave a half-hearted wave that I took to mean 'no'. I had a hollow feeling of incompleteness: her indifference quashed the sense of possibility – of exciting possibilities – beginning to take shape in my mind.

~ o ~

My surmise proved false: she came back. Not only that: she didn't leave.

A mistaken impression was easily formed of Carol on the basis of her clothes or her rustic blush. Those things were simply her cover; a travesty adopted by the bold heroine of a picaresque. She liked to drink and to be around when things were getting rowdy.

I took a joint from a happy guy, bare-chested with very long hair down to his pointy shoulder blades. Carol and I smoked the rest of it (which was most of it) then we stumble-danced and giggled, then we kissed; after that objects shed their specific properties and actions began to flow into each other. Somewhere in that time we fucked, more than once I have the impression. At some stage too, it became understood that Carol was coming back with us. I learned this from Massimo: 'Davey, you can ride back in the car with "la Carol". I fancy some fresh air; Paolo's Guzzi is a smoother ride than the fucking Simca...'

'OK! Yeah! Outstanding...' Listening to myself, I sounded like a kid; not at all like who I took myself to be. But those were the words that came out so who was I to argue? It was agreed: Carol was of our party and I was very happy.

3.

I willed her gently bobbing form to make some movement independent of the pull of the water. I am a cheerful optimist by nature – everyone I know has at some stage made a similar observation – but I was swept by a sense of dread, like a shape passing a window, already gone by the time you look up. Carol's catchphrase came back to me. 'You're a long time dead...' Fatalism seemed to hang like wet garments from her; it could never be put off. Uncertainty took root from these notions.

I called out loudly, in a voice I judged to be calm and measured, but probably wasn't at all so. There was no reaction out on the lake. I started to feel panic. I paced the water's edge whilst my mind cleared. My resolve sharpened. Then I took to the water.

Hunters

(Extract from 'Beauty on the Streets')

We dropped down off the top of a stony ridge, and found a hollow in the shelter of a brake of hazels, where we laid ourselves untidily amongst the parched grass. From the air, I thought, we must have looked like bodies flung hither and thither by some explosion.

This was a hunting trip. We had one gun between the four of us, a .22 belonging to Paolo. And we had achieved a 'bag', though the truth was that the well-conditioned rabbit we carried on our clumsy scramblings had met its end at daybreak, long before Omar, Massimo and myself had arrived. Paolo had spotted it from his window whilst shaving. The creature had been intent on its breakfast, the short greener grass under the olive in the yard, which on a vaporous autumn morning must have looked temptingly fresh.

'A good fat one, too lazy to move, just like Omar. I had time to go find some shells, load up, and it was *still* there eating itself silly, twenty metres away. I could have clubbed it.'

The hunting party, once constituted, had enjoyed less luck. We had attempted a few pot-shots at small birds, when they settled briefly in the bushes that softened these slopes — whose acute inclines had us doubling as we climbed. Rather, the others had taken shots. I couldn't reconcile myself to firing on birds, which, back in England, my mother would have encouraged to the bird-table. I had taken aim at a dove; I told myself it could just about be considered game, but the flock had taken wing as I fired. I was glad of the excuse for missing.

Omar had brought some beer. We also had a loaf of bread and, for some reason, a can of anchovies, but the main idea was to 'live off the country'; to kill our lunch and forage for mushrooms. We broached the beer well before midday, when we rested up under a clump of pines. The late morning sun was beginning to heat the land and release the scent of thyme.

'I'm shattered,' said Omar, stopping to make this announcement.

'Soft living. Look at the gut you're carrying,' said Paolo. For emphasis he slapped the portion of belly that shoved out between waistband and the 'Live at Monterey' T-shirt which, in fairness, was a size too small – something Omar elected to overlook because he claimed it had been worn by Hendrix. It was signed, giving rise to the objection that the great man surely did not write his name in his own shirts like a school kid.

'Sure he does. He's always giving his stuff away. He's not about possessions – 'this is mine all mine, that over there's yours'. All that private property shit's uncool; he's about sharing, sharing his gift, sharing his stuff…'

'So he writes his name in his own shirt – 'this shirt belongs to Jimi' – because possessions are so irrelevant – how's that figure?' Paolo was in an argumentative mood.

'You're so far offside, you don't get it at all. It wasn't 'his' shirt, in like a possessive kind of way. He just wore it for a time – maybe for a set, or a recording session, maybe only for an hour or two, who knows – maybe only for ten minutes, maybe only for a few seconds, or maybe-ee,' and it was clear Omar relished this possibility, 'he gave it to some chick he balled…'

'Share this, baby, share mah dick – then gave the chick a souvenir…'

'That's the kind of sharing I believe in…'. Massimo joined in to head off the argument that was gathering pace.

'I heard of this chick that takes plaster casts of guys' dicks…'

'How's that work? A load of wet plaster on your dick, you're not going to stay hard…'

'That's where you're wrong. Plaster gets hot when it's setting. Dipping your dick in plaster, man, that's a rare exotic pleasure…'

Omar took six bottles of beer out of his pack. It was a brand I had never seen elsewhere, paradoxically called *Favorit*. He got it through relatives in Jugoslavia. The idea had been to sell it cut-price to bars in the neighbourhood, except it had not been well received.

'Hey, man, I've been hauling the beer. That's what's killing me. And it would be a whole lot more use in me than in this fucking rucksack – so time to lighten the load. You can drink it or carry it, it's up to you.' With that he handed around the bottles he was carrying, contriving surreptitiously to shake up the beer he gave to Paolo, who habitually opened bottles with his teeth. Paolo duly popped the cap and released half the contents into his face. He flicked the remainder straight at Omar and gave chase.

'Hey, man, don't waste your beer, I carried that up this fucking mountain. Hey, man, it's not my fault, it must have…got shook up…man, it's hot, it's the heat, feel that sun…' Omar reeled out his excuses whilst maintaining a safe distance from Paolo's revenge.

'You're going to suffer, you fucker, get yourself back here – where your punishment awaits…'

'You know what, I love to walk in the mountains, the fresh air, the little birdies…' Omar filled his lungs like a fitness enthusiast taking deep breaths.

'Keep on walking, baby. I like a moving target.' Paolo took up the .22. He sighted and fired. A puff of earth and pine needles flicked up three yards to Omar's left. Dust hung in the air, drifting slowly on the breeze. Omar began to chortle like a gleeful infant.

'Hey, it's like a fucking manhunt. You're like the sheriff…I'm a mean hombre… just out…of the stockade…' He dived and rolled into cover. A shot crackled. It's passage was marked only by the click of a branch. Omar supplied a more fitting ricochet sound effect. 'Peeyyeowww.'

The game continued for a time, Omar taking cover behind different trees and eventually a boulder, and Paolo loosing off shots, trying to achieve suitably filmic effects. Real-life ballistics did not oblige.

We finished up the beer and moved on. The hunt gave way to target practice. We would each take a shot at some mark that one or other proposed – two rocks one on top of another, a discarded tomato can – until Paolo became sulky that we were using up his ammunition. Then we soldiered on in silence for a while, enjoying the sun but also noting the keen edge to the breeze as we climbed higher. Our goal was a lopsided mountain – hill really, except the others referred to these hills as mountains – with a section of sheer rock dropping away to one side of an elongated crest. According to Paolo, there were caves among the rocks. They would be worth exploring, the sort of place, Omar said, where there might be a stash of money from a bank job, or a haul of jewellery, or even some guy hiding out.

He may have been right for all I know, because we never gained that Eldorado. We were hungry. We found a sheltered spot, the hollow just off the crest of the ridge, and set about making a fire to cook the rabbit. Paolo took a clasp-knife and paunched it. The taut belly parted and guts slid neatly onto the ground at his feet. He reached inside and pulled out the heart, which settled like a toad in his open palm. He held out the ruddy jewel for our inspection, as if to say, 'take a good look, all your hopes and dreams depend on a little chunk of meat like so'.

Massimo stirred the guts with a stick. 'The guts of the last capitalist – now we just need the last bureaucrat so we can hang him, and be happy.' We laughed. The slogan was popular in Paris. The irony here in Italy was that half the country seemed to be in state employment, so the idea of there ever being a 'last' was pleasingly absurd.

'Does that go for apparatchiks, too?'

'For sure. Communists are the worst bureaucrats. *Politics is in the streets* – and in the factories, and the offices. Did you know, there have been one hundred million hours of strikes this autumn? That's what they are saying, and things are jacking up.'

'How do they know? Who's counting?' I had noticed the strikes and demonstrations, of course, but had missed out on the fact the actions were replicated across the country.

'It was in the *Struggle*. There's a garbage collection strike next week. That's going to make them think — tourists picking their way through piles of crap...'

'Yeah, they thought things would die down after their show of force...' said Paolo, looking up from his butchery.

'Now it's the The Hot Autumn – that's what the papers are all calling it.'

Omar helped peel the skin off the rabbit, holding onto the legs as Paolo tugged. The pelt came away finally with a wet tearing noise, revealing the lustrous beauty of the flayed muscles, still sheathed in a filmy membrane.

'Man, I could eat it just like that, I'm so hungry.'

'Fucking cannibal.'

'The bunny rabbit I could eat, not you, Davey. You got too may zits – which means your meat would only be fit for dog food.' Omar's hands were bloody. He went to smear me. I evaded him, and joined Massimo in the search for wood. We dropped down the hill into a fringe of undersized deciduous trees and soon began to find dead branches. Perhaps because it was a challenge, Massimo wanted the lower limb from a dead tree. We hung on it, bouncing with our feet off the ground, trying to get it to snap, but there was more strength left in it than appeared.

'So all the strikes, where's it going?'

'Well they are mainly about pay and conditions. The unions like to say they're setting the agenda, but they're not, not all the time anyway. Just as often it's local, the factories and workshops taking themselves out. Yeah, the spirit of 22nd September is still alive.' The date was the anniversary of the founding of the Italian Communist Party. Massimo gave the branch a last swing with all his body weight, both feet off the ground. 'Long live the twenty-second! Twenty two-two-two.' He hauled down on the beat of 'two'. The branch rustled and bent almost to the ground. 'Bollocks, that fucker's not going to give.'

'It's still a spontaneous thing, then?' It seemed to me things had changed since the suppression of the university sit-in; optimism had drained away.

'For sure. It's a spontaneous expression of grievances, there's no doubt about that, and there's no telling where it will go, that's why the politicos are nervous. It's easier for them when the big unions are running the show. This is not really a revolutionary movement, though. Small local demands can always be bought off. We are not involved, not directly. We're watching, of course. We express solidarity; we go to factory-gate demos and occupations when they happen. The main thing is the dialectical process. This is a transitional stage, a necessary historical transition We watch, and take a hand to keep the process going...'

'Waiting for the authorities to over-react?'

'Maybe. Who's to say how things will pan out?' Massimo gave a gentle smile. 'One thing's for sure: we are not trying to lay utopian notions on the workers; raise consciousness to correspond with our own ideas – that doesn't work. You've got to acknowledge the tide of history. You can't control it, you just have to judge your moment. Like this branch: it'll fall off – just not today, not under our weight.'

Massimo's tune had changed. Before he had been for the great popular consensus, the continuous democratic reinvention of society starting at the grass roots. Now he seemed to have grown circumspect, which maybe meant smarter too. I couldn't help wondering: who were the 'we' that he referred to?

We went back with an armful of sticks each. I made a cone of twigs and set fire to them with my Zippo. Paolo had spitted the rabbit and stuffed it full of sage leaves. There was nothing to do but wait. Massimo had brought a joint which, not trusting conditions on the ground for such an operation, he had thoughtfully rolled back at No. 17. We lay back like pashas, inhaling and catching wafts of aromatic meat on the breeze.

'I've heard they've got dossiers, just like the police.'

'That's heavy. What's in them?' The talk had turned to the MSI, the current incarnation of the Fascist party. Omar had launched the subject and seemed for him, unusually bothered by the rumour of the dossiers. I thought back to the 'Milk Tray men' at the occupation. It was true the MSI were not harmless nutters.

'People's names.'

'Whose? Yours, mine, Mickey Mouse?'

'Everyone on the left. All the memberships of parties, especially the Autonomy; anyone carrying a union card, anyone on the police files…'

'That's half the population! They aren't that organised, for fuck's sake – most of them can't read, you can't see them keeping records…' There was laughter. Paolo's was a fair point, but there was no denying that the MSI had been active. They had been on the streets, having organised counter-demonstrations to coincide with some of the bigger strikes.

Omar stood up and took the joint from Paolo. He took a pull, then stood gesturing with it, like a man with a cigar holding forth after dinner. 'They beat up that guy from Fountain Street. He was a strike organiser. They just waited for him to come home and beat him up outside his house.'

'That's terrible, real bad...'

'It's bad but it doesn't amount to systematic persecution of the left...'

'There were some of them hanging around outside our place...'

'C'mon, a couple of tokes and the paranoia sets in...'

'Believe me, I know them. I knew one of them from school. He was a little bastard – he'd always grass on you to the teachers. Look, they've got lists of people, just like Costa said in Greece. Bosses just hand over the names of trouble-makers, money changes hands and...' Omar made a hand-washing gesture, skimming his palms together.

'So what? You want us to go out and beat some of them up? And then what? They...'

Omar still had the joint. He used it to drive home his point. 'No, no, better than that. Here's my idea. Their place is out on the ring-road, right? It's kind of on its own, an administration office and a meeting room...'

'And a wanking room...'

'The Chapel of Onan where they worship...'

'Oh Lord of the five-fingered shuffle...'

'Give me light for I am made blind...'

'Yeah. That's it. That's the total 'it-ness' of the 'it'. Yeah, we light them up,' Omar continued, intent on laying out his plan despite interruptions. 'We go along one night and post a Molotov through their window. Paff. Let there be light. Paff. No more list.' Omar danced around the fire, intoxicated by his vision of conflagration and vengeance. I exchanged glances with Paolo. I guess the same thought passed through both our minds. The scheme was crazy but temptingly feasible. I began to giggle.

Paolo looked across to Massimo, sitting cross-legged, stirring the fire. 'What do you reckon, Massimo?'

Massimo rose and recovered the joint from Omar. He took a long drag, waited and exhaled. His eyes narrowed. He was smiling. His smile was like a philosophical state that he inhabited. 'I'll talk to people.'

'People? You don't need an army. We could do it, the four of us...'

Massimo looked at me sharply. 'It's a political action. It has to be discussed...' His body sagged and he fell back spread-eagled, staring at the sky. 'Discussed... from a di-a-lectical perspective.' He giggled, or maybe I did.

We devoured the rabbit, and the bread, and the sardines, and a pack of Tic Tacs, in what seemed like a few seconds. We were inadequately provisioned and still hungry. There were vineyards lower down the hill, with ripe grapes hanging on the vines, temptingly succulent.

Hunting was over for the day.

'You've got to be up with the lark to bag yourself a meal. Afternoon is no use,' said Paolo. 'The birdies like to siesta, same as us.'

A siesta sounded good, if only it were preceded by something more to eat. We headed back down the hill, sustained by an identical thought: that Paolo's pantry was supplied with pasta and beer and cans of this and that. The sun was hot on our backs. We were still high and laughing.

~ About the Author ~

Chris Bruce is a visual artist who lives and works in Cornwall, UK.

He exhibits as a painter, photographer and installationist; his paintings are in private collections. He is also a political cartoonist whose daily drawings can be found on Instagram at *bruce_works15*.

More recently, he has turned to writing, which he explains as follows: 'You reach a moment in life where you start to see things through a new lens — become *retrospective*.'

Graduating originally in Modern Languages from Cambridge University, Chris Bruce lived for several years in Italy, where he worked as a teacher. His stories are set in that country, and concerned with the political undercurrents surrounding the youth movement of the 1960's and '70's.

He says: 'I see the same themes being played out again today. There's a popular move against a *status quo* that, for a long while, has seemed immovable. People are taking to the streets again to make their voices heard.'

'Falling' is his first work of fiction to be issued. It will be followed by a full length novel, 'Beauty on the Streets', and a sequel, 'On Wings of Lead'.

Readers — a request before you go: by leaving a review, you can assist other readers to discover this book. Your help in this way is hugely appreciated. Thank you so much!

Printed in Poland
by Amazon Fulfillment
Poland Sp. z o.o., Wrocław

61941981R00047